ZOMBIE!

TOMMY DONBAVAND

With illustrations by
Tom Percival

Barrington Stoke

For the real Jake, Nathan and Olivia –
who are not nearly as frightening!

First published in 2009 in Great Britain by
Barrington Stoke Ltd
18 Walker Street, Edinburgh, EH3 7LP

www.barringtonstoke.co.uk

Reprinted 2014

Text © 2009 Tommy Donbavand
Illustrations © Tom Percival

A CIP catalogue record for this book is available
from the British Library upon request

ISBN: 978-1-84299-708-6

Printed in China by Leo

Contents

Chapter 1
It Started with a Scream

My grandad died when I was nine.

He always picked me up from school on Fridays because that's the day my mum works late. Every week we'd buy ice-creams and eat them on the way home. Then we'd rent a movie and watch it and eat popcorn until mum got home. Then one Friday, Mum met me at the school gates, not Grandad. She looked very sad, and she said that Grandad had died of a heart attack at lunch-time. His funeral was a week later. I miss him.

I've always visited his grave. I like doing that. Some of the kids at school say the grave-yard is spooky, but to me it's just a nice place I can come to and visit my grandad. I talk to him in his grave. I know it's just a grave-stone with his name on it, but I like telling him what I've been doing. At first I felt a bit silly when I talked to a lump of stone, but now it feels fine – almost like when he was here.

My name is Nathan. My sister's Olivia. She was only a baby when Grandad died. She doesn't remember him at all. Sometimes I take her to the grave-yard with me. I try to make her say hello and talk, but she always skips off to look at the flowers people have put on the other graves. She can be really girly sometimes. I don't mind. When she's gone, I can say things to Grandad that I don't

want her to hear. Like what my best friend, Simon, gets up to.

"He nicked Emma Peel's bag at break time and wrote on her pencil case that she loves Chris Jones!" I said. "She went mad when she got her pencil case out in maths and everyone saw it."

I brushed a few dead leaves off the grave-stone as I talked. It was the middle of October and it was starting to get dark early. I knew I'd have to get Olivia home soon or my mum would go on at me for keeping her out late.

"Emma started shouting at Simon right in the middle of class!" I said. Thinking about what happened made me grin. "Mr Parker made her tell why she was so upset. Then he sent Simon out of the classroom but he was smiling about it too. I think the only person who didn't think it was funny was ..."

SCREAM!

I jumped when I heard the noise. The scream had come from far away. Maybe it was kids playing on the estate. The scream gave me a fright but I was glad it stopped me talking. It was getting very dark. We needed to get home quickly.

"Olivia!" I shouted. "We have to get going!" Normally Olivia played at the top of the grave-yard where there were some big trees and a rose bed. I looked for her there but I couldn't see her.

I began to panic. Where was she? My little sister can be a pain when she comes into my room and touches my stuff, but I didn't want anything bad to happen to her. And what's more, mum would kill me if I lost her.

SCREAM!

That scream wasn't from the estate. It came from the old part of the grave-yard. I always told Olivia not to go over there because the ground was bumpy. She could fall and hurt herself. *Is that what had happened?* I asked myself.

I ran across the grave-yard, to and fro between the grave-stones. What colour was Olivia's dress? Everything looked grey as it got darker but I knew I'd see something that was pink or yellow. There was nothing.

I scrambled round the big oak tree and then I saw her. She was standing near a huge grave in the shape of an angel and looking hard at the ground. I raced across to her.

"Where have you been?" I asked. "I've told you not to come to this bit of the grave-yard!"

My sister was shaking. Her eyes were big and wide and she pointed at something in the mud. "It's a leg!" she croaked.

I peered down at the ground. It was hard to see anything at all. "Don't be stupid!" I said. "That's just an old bit of wood. Now come on!"

As I dragged her away from the angel, a hand burst out of the ground and grabbed my ankle. This time we both screamed!

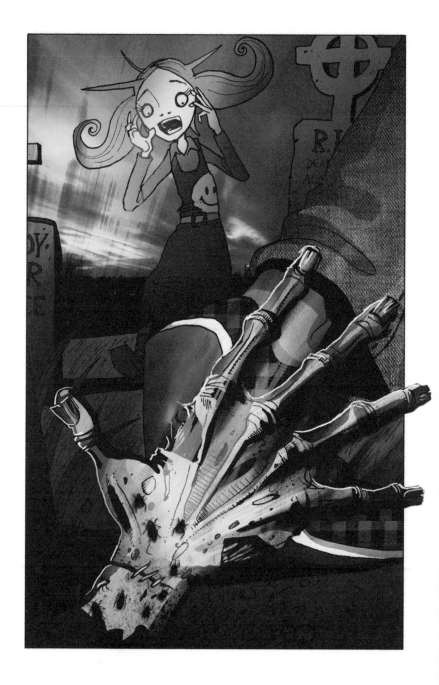

Chapter 2
Zombie Attack!

The hand around my ankle was made of rotting flesh. The nails were broken and black with dirt. Tiny insects crawled around the wrist. It pulled me down to the ground but I kept kicking at the fingers with my other foot. Olivia was screaming again.

I heard some bones break and suddenly my ankle was free. I jumped up and ran. I was quite far away when I saw that Olivia wasn't with me. I dashed back and took her hand to pull her away, but she wouldn't move. She was frozen to the spot, watching a thin shape push out of the grave.

The person was made up of lots of different body parts. The hand that had grabbed me was a man's hand, but the other arm had a smaller, woman's hand with red finger-nails at the end of it.

As more of the thing pushed up out of the ground, I saw that its legs were different too. One was short and stocky, the other long and thin. The thing brushed the dirt off its old, grubby suit and limped towards us, with its arms stretched out. Suddenly I knew what this thing was – a zombie!

"GLARK!" The creature made a wet, glugging sound as it lurched towards us. I grabbed a big bit of wood that lay on the ground and pushed Olivia behind me. I swung the wood round and hit the zombie on the head. The monster nearly fell over but somehow stayed on its feet and went on walking towards us.

"GLARK!"

I looked around me. I needed something else to use as a weapon. But the only things left were the old grave-stones that stuck out of the ground.

That was it! I had an idea. I ran as fast as I could at the zombie and pushed it hard in the chest. My hands slipped through the rotten material of its jacket and sank into the soft skin of the monster's ribs.

The zombie fell back and tripped over a broken grave-stone. It crashed to the ground. Bones cracked as it tumbled. "GLARK!" it shouted.

I stared down at my hands in the dim light. There was some sort of brown goo from the zombie's chest all over them. I tried hard not to think about what the stuff was. I rubbed my fingers on my jeans, then grabbed Olivia's hand again.

As we started to run, the zombie got back to its feet and came after us. Was there any way to stop this thing? Olivia and I zig-zagged between the grave-stones until we could see the grave-yard gates. I let go of her hand and pushed the gates hard. They didn't move. While we had been fighting with the zombie, someone had locked us in!

"GLARK!"

I spun round. The zombie was lurching towards us, arms stretched out in front of it. I could just see the big hole I'd made in its chest as its jacket flapped in the breeze.

"What do you want with us?" I shouted. "Why can't you leave us alone?"

"GLARK!"

Olivia began to cry as the zombie came closer and closer. I looked up at the graveyard gates to see if there was any way we could climb over them to escape. They were too high. Maybe I could get over them, but Olivia was too small and there was no way I was leaving her behind.

I turned back towards the zombie and got ready to fight. I wasn't going to give in easily. "Come on, then!" I yelled and I put up my fists.

"GLARK! GLARK!" The zombie bent over as it made the disgusting wet noise over and over again. Suddenly, a big fat slug shot out of its mouth and landed on the grass with a 'plop'!

The zombie stood up straight. "That's better!" it said. "I've been trying to get rid of that thing for days!"

I stared as the thing twisted its face into a weird smile. Olivia was so surprised that she stopped crying.

"Now," said the zombie. "Do you know where I would be able to buy twenty bottles of lemonade?"

Chapter 3
Meet Jake

"Lemonade?" I asked. "Why would a zombie want to buy twenty bottles of lemonade?" Was I being rude? Maybe I should start again. "Excuse me," I said. "Can I call you 'zombie', or would you prefer 'dead person'?"

The thing smiled. Its mouth was full of maggots. "Zombie is fine," it said. "Or you can call me Jake. That's my name, after all."

"Hello, Jake," said Olivia, and she held her hand out to the zombie. I slapped her wrist away before the monster could shake it.

"Good idea," said Jake. "I've been loaded with diseases for tens of years now." He held his bent and twisted fingers up to look at them. "And, it might be a bit hard to shake hands with broken fingers."

I suddenly felt bad that I'd kicked the zombie's hand so hard. "Sorry," I muttered.

"No problem!" said Jake. "I can always change them." He grabbed hold of his wrist and, with a horrible squelch, he ripped away the hand with the broken fingers. For a moment, I thought I was going to be sick.

The zombie tossed the useless hand out of the way and pushed his good arm into the ground. When he pulled it out again he was holding another hand. "These things are just lying round down there!" he said with a big grin.

I'd had pizza for school lunch and it flopped in my belly again as Jake licked his wrist bone and shoved the new hand onto the end of his arm. There were a few cracks and clicks then, seconds later, the fingers were wiggling as if they'd always been there.

Olivia's mouth dropped open. "How do you do that?" she asked.

Jake gave a shrug. "Dunno," he replied. "Some kind of zombie magic, I guess. There has to be some good things about being dead!"

"So, you really are dead?" I said.

"Dead as a door-nail!" grinned Jake. He rapped his chest where his heart should have been. "This thing hasn't pumped in over sixty years."

"Sixty years!" gasped Olivia. "How did you die?"

"Olivia!" I snapped. "That's rude!" I gave her a warning look but in fact, I was just as keen to know how Jake had died.

"It was the war," said Jake.

"Were you a soldier?" I asked.

"I was," said Jake. "But that's not how I died. The funny thing was, after months fighting the enemy, I came home for a week's holiday and a bomb dropped on my house. I died in my own bed." He pulled open his shirt to show the hole my hand had sunk into. "The bomb hit me right here!"

My stomach churned again as I peered into the sticky brown hole. My hand had just been in there!

"It must be horrible!" said Olivia.

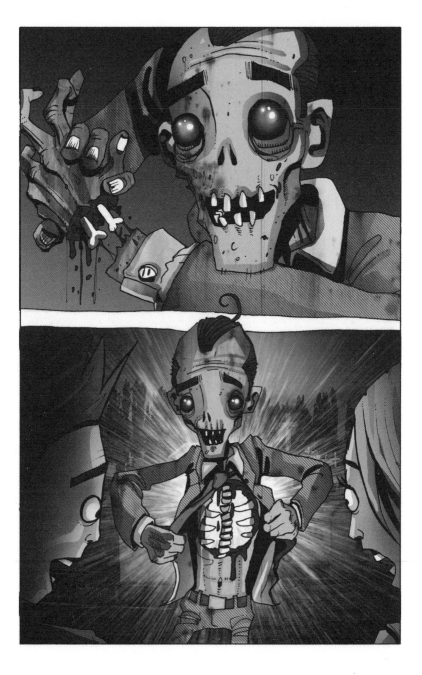

"Being dead?" said Jake. "Not at all. I've got more friends than I ever had when I was alive. I've got tons of free time and the parties are fantastic!"

"Parties?" I asked. "Zombies have parties?"

"Any chance we get!" said Jake. "That's why I'm here now. There's a big do on tonight – the grave-yard is 200 years old. That's why the other guys gave me all their best body bits. They've asked me to go out to get the lemonade, sausage rolls and jelly babies."

"Zombies eat sausage rolls!" I said. "I must be dreaming!"

"I'm no dream," said Jake. "But I think you should be in bed soon – it's very dark."

I looked up at the sky. It was dark now and the only light was from a full, white moon. "Mum's going to kill me!" I moaned. "I have to ring her right now!"

"You're right. Mum'll be really mad at us," said Olivia. Then she grabbed my hand and dragged me back to the grave-yard gates. "Come on, Nathan!"

"And I can't stand here chatting all night," grinned Jake. "Those jelly babies won't buy themselves!" He zapped the gates with a little more of his zombie magic, and they swung open wide.

"Just try not to scare anyone else!" I said as the zombie limped away. Too late! As Olivia and I put our hands up to wave we heard another scream.

Chapter 4
The Supermarket

I felt bad telling mum a lie, but it was Olivia's idea.

"If you tell her we're hanging out with a zombie, she'll think you're messing about and tell us to come home right now!" Olivia said. "Let's tell her we're going trick-or-treating."

"But, it's not Halloween for another two weeks," I said.

"So? We're starting early this year!"

I sighed and rang home. I promised Mum I'd look after Olivia and that we'd be at the grave-yard gates in an hour for her to pick us up. Now all we had to do was work out where Jake had gone.

SCREAM!

"He's down there!" I said as Olivia and I chased after the sound. By the time we'd caught up with our un-dead friend, he was half-way along the street.

"For someone with odd legs, you sure can move fast!" I said, panting hard.

Jake grinned. "I haven't been out in the fresh air for years," he said. "This might be the only chance I get to enjoy a good walk!"

"Do zombies go for walks often?" asked Olivia.

"All the time," said Jake. "If ever you see someone in the street who looks as if they don't belong there, I expect that's a zombie."

My head was spinning. "We've been walking round with zombies for years?" I asked.

"Most likely," said Jake.

"But how come we can't tell," I said. "Zombies have dead flesh and rotting skin – like you've got!"

"Most days, it's the young ones who go out to get stuff," said Jake. "They're just letting me go this time because I wouldn't stop asking!"

"Who's they?" asked Olivia.

"The zombies in charge," replied Jake. "The people that got buried first are always in charge of their grave-yard."

SCREAM!

A woman who was walking towards us spotted Jake's rotten face in the street-light and turned pale. She grabbed on to the lamp post and looked as if she was going to faint.

"Trick or treat!" Olivia shouted out happily. "What do you think of my dad's zombie costume?"

The woman looked better right away. "Oh!" she said. "A costume! Of course! It's great!" Jake grinned.

"Here you are, little girl!" added the woman and she handed Olivia a pound coin. "Get yourself some sweets!" With one last look at Jake, she hurried away, laughing to herself for being so scared.

I looked at my sister. I was shocked "You just lied to that woman and got a pound out of it!"

Olivia smiled at me. "I'm not as cute and goody-goody as everyone thinks, Nathan!" she said. "I only wear these pretty little dresses to trick people." She turned and skipped away, flicking her hair from side to side.

"She's good!" said Jake.

"She's not the sister I know!" I added.

"She seems to be able to look after hers–" The zombie stopped talking and stared up at the block of flats at the end of the street.

"What's the matter?" I asked.

"The corner shop," groaned Jake. "It's gone!"

"There used to be a shop here?" asked Olivia, as she skipped back to us. "These flats have been here ever since I can remember."

Jake slumped to the ground. "I'm an idiot," he said. "A stupid, dead idiot! Why did I expect a grotty old corner shop to still be here for me sixty years after I died? Of course they were going to knock it down!"

The zombie sighed. "I've let everyone down," he said. "I was so excited at the chance to climb out of my grave that I didn't think to ask the newer zombies where I should go to buy the party food!"

I looked across the street to the bright lights of the supermarket. "Well," I said. "There's always that place ..." I pointed out.

Chapter 5
Z-Alert

The security guard spotted us the minute we walked in. He was standing near the computers and TVs, playing a gruesome game on a PlayStation.

He had a radio on his belt. He pulled it out and pressed a button on the side. He spoke slowly. "This is Clint at station alpha," he said. "We have a Z-Alert. I repeat, a Z-Alert!"

After a second, the boss spoke back. "Clint," we heard him say. "We don't have a Z-Alert. You're by the computer games, where you always are. And you've got to stop making up your own secret language. None of us know what a 'Z-Alert' is!"

Clint scowled at the radio for a moment, then clipped it back onto his belt. "Looks like I'm acting alone on this mission!" he said. I watched as he spun to switch off the computer. And that's when I saw the game he'd been playing. I knew that game!

I hurried to catch up with Jake and Olivia. An old man had just given her another trick-or-treat pound coin. "We've got a problem!" I said.

"He gave me this pound because Jake's costume is so good!" said Olivia.

"I don't mean that problem!" I snapped. I knew I would have to have a talk with my sister later about how she was making all that Halloween money. I knew I'd never believe a word she said ever again. But that wasn't the problem right now. "The security guard was playing *Un-dead Attack*," I shouted.

Jake and Olivia stared at me. They didn't have a clue what I meant.

"*Un-dead Attack*," I said again. "It's a game where you have to kill zombies! And now that guard's coming this way!" I looked back down the supermarket and I saw Clint edge his way towards us. He saw me look at him and quickly pretended to be reading what it said on nappies.

I don't know why our supermarket even needs a security guard. The only theft from the store was when two stray dogs ran in last Christmas and ate a packet of sausages. That made the front page of the local paper –

'Hot Dogs for Cold Dogs'. Well done to the person who wrote that one!

Jake bent down to whisper. "Do you think he's seen me?" he asked.

I blinked. Jake's breath was awful. It stung my eyes. I looked back at Jake. "He's always playing that stupid zombie game and now he's reading the list of things that are in a jar of baby food, so I'd say yes."

"Come on then," said Olivia and grabbed a shopping trolley. "Let's get everything Jake needs and get out of here." She began to push the trolley to the frozen foods fridges. I followed her and Jake limped along beside me.

We hurried around the bread shelves to the freezers. I looked back and saw Clint peering through a shelf piled high with tins of baked beans. He was definitely following us!

I spotted the sausage rolls and grabbed the handle of the trolley. "What are you doing?" Olivia wanted to know. "I'm pushing!"

"Don't be daft!" I growled. "I'm older, it's better if I push!"

"I found the trolley!" Olivia said. "I'm pushing, and you're looking after Jake!"

I pulled her fingers off the trolley handle. Little sisters can be so stupid sometimes. The security guard had almost caught up to us and she was arguing about who should push the shopping trolley.

"I'm pushing!" I shouted, and shoved her to one side.

Olivia fell against a rack of chocolate muffins and started to cry. Clint had stopped pretending to read food labels and stood watching us. He looked angry. How could this get any worse?

And that's when Jake's leg fell off.

Chapter 6
Trolley Dash

For a moment, everyone just stared at the leg lying on the floor with no owner. Even Olivia stopped crying. Then, everything went crazy ...

"Stop right there!" shouted Clint. I looked up and saw him pull something from his belt and point it at me. He had a gun! Since when did supermarkets let their security guards carry guns?

I threw four packets of sausage rolls into the shopping trolley, then grabbed Jake and lifted him off the ground. He was a lot lighter than I expected but then he was just skin and bone.

"Aren't you worried about catching a disease?" the zombie asked.

"Trust me," I replied. "A zombie disease is fun and games next to what'll happen if they catch us and ring my mum!" I dumped Jake in the shopping trolley and pushed it as fast as I could. "Olivia, get the leg!" I shouted.

As Olivia bent to pick up Jake's leg, Clint ran towards her. She stood and swung the leg round as hard as she could. She bashed the security guard on the chin with its foot. Clint crashed backwards into a stack of cornflakes boxes.

"We're going to have a serious talk when all this is over!" I said as Olivia ran up and tossed Jake his missing leg.

The zombie licked the leg stub and pressed it back into the messy open hole at his hip. Nothing happened. He licked again, and this time his face got yellow goo on it. I tried my hardest not to look. Still the leg wouldn't stick on.

"What's wrong?" I asked as we skidded round the corner to the fizzy drinks. "Why isn't your leg sticking?"

"I don't know!" said Jake. "The zombie magic isn't working! Maybe we're too far away from the grave-yard."

I dragged the trolley to a stop and began to throw bottles of lemonade in on top of the zombie. "OK," I said, "but why did your leg fall off in the first place?"

"It's too warm in here," said Jake. "The grave-yard is always nice and cold, even in the summer." As he spoke, there was a sound like someone pouring out a jug of custard, and the zombie's left arm slipped away from his body. "I need to get somewhere cold as quickly as possible!"

"We could put him in one of the freezers," Olivia said.

I heard a noise and glanced over my shoulder. Clint was on his feet and was running towards us again. He held the gun in one hand and was brushing cornflakes out of his hair with the other. "I don't think we'll be here long enough to use the freezers," I shouted. I dumped the last lemonade bottles into the trolley and pushed it down to the check-out. "Anyway – what would happen if someone came in for a packet of fish fingers and went home with human fingers instead!"

"Jelly babies!" yelled Jake as we passed the sweets display.

"We're going too fast to stop!" I shouted. I was pushing the trolley at full speed. "We'll have to go round again!"

"The security guard is right behind us!" screamed Olivia.

"Then help me push!" I yelled.

My sister and I gripped the handle of the shopping trolley and ran as fast as we could. Shoppers dived out of our way. I was just happy that we were moving too quickly for them to see the rotting face in the middle of all the bottles of fizzy drink and packets of sausage rolls.

"We'll have to slow down!" shouted Olivia.

"We can't!" I said, looking back at Clint. He was red in the face and panting, but he still had the gun in his hand and he was catching us up. "Faster!"

It turned out Olivia was right. We did have to slow down to take the corner but because I thought I knew best, we didn't. As we turned the trolley around the rack of CDs, the wheels on one side went up into the air. I struggled to hold onto the trolley handle as the heavy lemonade bottles tipped it over. It was no good.

Olivia and I crashed to the ground as the trolley flipped. We landed among squashed sausage rolls, exploding bottles of lemonade and – worst of all – about a thousand zombie body parts.

Chapter 7
Party

Jake had totally fallen apart. His hands and feet lay all over the floor which was sticky with spilled lemonade. His head had wedged itself in between two bottles of washing-up liquid on a nearby shelf.

"Ow!" he said.

"Freeze, monster-lovers!" Clint shouted. He stood over us, gun pointed right at me. He looked around at the different bits of Jake. "I knew you had a zombie with you the moment I saw you!"

"So, what are you going to do now?" Olivia wanted to know. "Shoot us?"

"Olivia!" I hissed.

"I might shoot!" said Clint.

"Go on, then!" my sister went on. "See if we care!"

"Olivia, shut up!" I snapped. The gun was pointing right at me, after all.

"I'm going to do it!" yelled Clint. His fingers squeezed tight around the gun.

"I dare you!" said Olivia.

With a roar, Clint pulled the trigger. I closed my eyes. Was I going to be the next dead body in the grave-yard? But there was no gun blast, and no bullets shot through the air towards me. Nothing happened. Well, almost nothing. I did get a bit of a wet face.

I opened my eyes. "That's a water pistol!" I said.

Olivia nodded. "I saw that's what it was right away," she said. "You had the same one when you were about ten."

I stared up at Clint. He was blushing now that everyone knew the secret of his gun. "What sort of man runs round with a water pistol?" I asked myself. I began to laugh.

"That's not important!" he shouted and he tucked the plastic toy back into his belt. "The important thing is that I'm going to have you two arrested. You've brought a zombie with you into a supermarket without permission!"

"And what about us?" said someone behind Clint. "Do we have to have permission to be here as well?"

Clint slowly turned round. There were almost a hundred other zombies standing behind him. Men and women all starting to rot and fall to bits stood in a crowd near the check-out. Each one of them had loads of scabs and sores, and most of them were missing eyes, ears and lips.

At the front of the group was someone I knew. He had a dusty old suit on. His skin was tighter than I remembered it, but the smile was still the same.

"Grandad!" I said.

"Hello, Nathan!" smiled my grandad. "Good to see you again." He turned to my sister. For the first time that night Olivia couldn't think of a thing to say. "You must be

little Olivia. You've really grown since the last time I saw you."

"Grandad," I said. It was hard to even say that. "I've been coming to visit you …"

"I know," said my grandad, "I listen to every word you say. Your mate Simon's been getting himself into a lot of trouble these days!"

The rest of the zombies laughed when Grandad said my best friend's name. "That thing with the pencil case was brilliant!" came a tiny voice from the back of the group.

"Now, just hold on a minute!" shouted Clint. He looked from zombie face to zombie face. I could see he was really scared. "I don't know what you're all talking about, but this is a Z-Alert, and I'm taking control!"

"How many times do I have to tell you that there is no such thing as a 'Z-Alert'!"

came a shout. The boss had come into the shop now and was staring at all the mess. "What on earth has happened here?"

Before Clint could open his mouth, my grandad shuffled up to him. "I'll tell you what happened," he said. "We're having an early Halloween party – as you can see, we're already in costume. My grand-children came in to pick up some sausage rolls and lemonade and your security guard here charged in. I don't know why – he thinks we're real zombies!"

The supermarket boss glared at Clint. "What?!" he roared.

"N-no!" the security guard began to say. "You don't understand ..."

"The only thing I don't understand is why you're not cleaning up this mess!" shouted the boss. He looked up at Jake's head, still stuck between the bottles of washing-up liquid. "And help that poor gentleman out of there. His head's come right through from the other side of the shelf!"

Clint's mouth opened and closed a few times as the boss marched off, but no words came out. At last, he gave a sigh and began to pick up the bits of smashed sausage roll.

Olivia grabbed some carrier bags from a checkout, and helped me to collect up the parts of Jake's body. "Will you be OK in there?" I asked as I put his head into one of the bags.

"I'll be fine," Jake smiled. "Once we're back at the grave-yard, it'll be cold enough for the zombie magic to hold me together again – then it's time to party!" Olivia took the carrier bags and dashed off to pay for the lemonade with her trick or treat money.

"Fancy one of these?" someone asked me. I turned to find my grandad standing behind me, with two ice-creams in his hand. They were the same ones we ate on the days Mum worked late and he collected me from school.

"I miss this," I said. I took one of the ice-creams and tried not to cry. "I miss you."

"I've never been far away," Grandad said, and messed my hair. "Let's catch up with Olivia." So my grandad and I walked out into the night, eating ice-cream and chatting – just like we'd always done.

Our books are tested
for children and young people by
children and young people.

Thanks to everyone who consulted on
a manuscript for their time and effort in
helping us to make our books better
for our readers.

Also by *Tommy Donbavand*...

Virus

"You only get viruses if you click on links you don't know, stupid," Nahim hissed. "But you've given me an idea ..."

When Nahim sends a virus to Polly and Amina, he has no idea that all three of them will be dragged inside the Internet.

How will they get home? How will they fight the virus? Who can help them?

If only Nahim's ICT class partner Max was good with computers ...

Uniform

"Hey, the piece of scum has got a school uniform!" Chadwick yelled. Bates and Wilson laughed. I know I should have felt embarrassed, or even scared. But I didn't. For some reason I wasn't scared today. In fact, I felt so good that I walked right over to him.

When Matt's mum buys him an old school uniform in a charity shop the tables are turned on the bullies. But what's with the uniform? And how far will it make Matt go?

More *Barrington Stoke* titles...

Young Werewolf
CORNELIA FUNKE

When Matt and his best friend Lisa encounter a strange beast in a dark alley, Matt's life changes for ever.

As the moon rises, Matt looks in the mirror and sees flashing yellow eyes and a LOT of hair!

Even Lisa doesn't have an answer to this crisis. As the full moon approaches, the wolf inside Matt is growing wilder and wilder ...

Ninja: First Mission
CHRIS BRADFORD

He waits under the floor-boards. He's been hidden for over an hour, lying still as a stone. His name is Taka. This is his first mission as a ninja and he must not fail ...

When the Grandmaster sends Taka on a special mission, this is his last chance to prove himself. But the mission is dangerous. To fail is to die, and Taka has failed before ...

Hagurosan
DARREN SHAN

Hagurosan wanted to stay at home and play. But his mother asked him to take cake to the spirits of the shrine. And so he pulled a face, stuck the cake in his pocket, and set off.

Hagurosan only meant to take a tiny bite of the cake. But then there was nothing left ...

The spirits have cursed people for less. What will they do to Hagurosan?

Young Wizards
MICHAEL LAWRENCE

Birthdays are great. You get gifts, and cake, and sometimes a party. Shame the next birthday is your sister's!

Say hello to Brin and Arlo, their stressed-out parents and their big sister Ellie. Ellie is about to be 13, which may be lucky for her ... or not. And Brin and Arlo have just discovered some interesting gifts of thier own.

www.barringtonstoke.co.uk